When the Night Owl Screams

By Michael H. Hanson

MoonDream
PRESS
An Imprint of Copper Dog Publishing, LLC

When The Night Owl Screams

Copyright ©2017 Copper Dog Publishing, LLC

Published by Moondream Press, an imprint of Copper Dog Publishing, LLC
537 Leader Circle, Louisville, CO 80027

Visit our Web site: www.copperdogpublishing.com

Credits:
Cover and Interior Design: Helen H. Harrison
Written by Michael H. Hanson

Cover art: Moon Maiden—2016,
Copyright ©Chris Mars/Chris Mars Publishing, Inc.
www.chrismarspublishing.com

Library of Congress Control Number: 2017957871
ISBN: 978-1-943690-16-9 Print
ISBN: 978-1-943690-17-6 Kindle

First Edition: October 2017

All poems Copyright ©2017 Moondream Press, an imprint of Copper Dog Publishing LLC

Cannoneer – originally published in Paradox Magazine, ©2005 Paradox Magazine

Fear—originally published in Autumn Blush, ©2007 Racket River Press.

Fire, I Dreamed, and *A Lovers' Tale*—originally published in *Jubilant Whispers,* ©2010 Racket River Press.

When The Night Owl Screams – originally published in the Blood and Spades Column, Official Newsletter of the HWA, ©2016 Horror Writers Association

Mister Deadsmile – originally published in the HWA Poetry Showcase Volume III, ©2016 Horror Writers Association

Printed in the United States of America

Interior art: *By Those Who Wreck*—2012, *The Dimming Room*—2001, *Freedom Translation of Cleared Resident Lincoln*—2000, *Doctor Quell*—1999, *Harvesting in the Lull*—2011, *The Looker*—2000
Copyright ©Chris Mars/Chris Mars Publishing, Inc.
www.chrismarspublishing.com

TABLE OF CONTENTS

CHAPTER SIX 123

ACKNOWLEDGMENTS

The poet wishes to thank:

Poet and Author Alessandro Manzetti for writing the excellent Introduction to this anthology.

Graphic Artist Helen Harrison for designing the front and back covers, as well as all interior layouts.

Artist Chris Mars for his chilling painting, *Moon Maiden*, used on the Cover, and his six macabre, black and white illustrations which grace each of the six chapters.

All of the fans and readers whose enthusiastic reaction to *DARK PARCHMENTS: Midnight Curses And Verses* convinced the poet to write and compile this second anthology of dark poetry.

INTRODUCTION

by Alessandro Manzetti

ACCOMPANYING SOME BRILLIANT poetic imagery by Michael, I read his latest dark collection of verses drinking a glass of Malbec wine, watching Saturn, up there, between the curves of space, gray and old like we're all becoming, more or less quickly.

Diving into these pages, savoring the Argentine aftertaste of my usual vino, and the French smooth flavor that Michael instilled into my senses, seasoned with a grenade of Apollinaire's thoughts, from my porch I hear the sound of an old ice cream truck.

As they hadn't in years, childhood memories came to visit me again, dressed in orange, with the blouse held tight with plaster buttons and clumps of grass between the toes. It was her, the past, like I remembered, running toward me with a chocolate ice cream clutched in her little hand, dripping down her legs and scraped knees.

At one point, she knelt close to me and dropped some bread crumbs on my pants: a cascade of memories rolled on my thighs forming a precise geometry, a constellation, no… a map; but where would it like to drive me? Maybe where I'm already going to without realizing it? Or elsewhere?

This is the secret of Michael's book: his intimately varnished poems carry us back and forth in time and space, as if you're sitting on a bus with the number zero alight on its iron muzzle.

The windows let the past unroll on their slippery sides, then in some long dark gallery hides the landscape that mirrors your face, deforming it, making it grotesque as happens in some of Luna Park's magic funhouse rooms. As you stretch your neck like an elastic band, and your skull grows bigger, widening like that of a tyrannosaurus rex, time stops, light comes back, and you're forced to anchor your gaze to that stranger horizon, out there, with its white bumps and the regular teeth of eternity's many possible gates. How many mouths does the Future have?

Among the tasty red berries and the darkest bitter ones I've gathered during this reading, keeping them in my pocket for tomorrow, you have to try: *Mother Daemon, Street Specter, Mister Deadsmile, Gather, The Scary Bazaar, Automaton, Heat Dome, Stranger Things, In the Mirror, The Projectionist's Poem, Duck!, She Was Sad But Filled With Mojo, At The Carnival,* and *Listen To The Pimp.*

This book is like a magical ticket to visit everything that has been, that touched and surrounded us, from yesterday's vanilla smell to that of chopped alien almonds of lost days, stuck inside us.

But for every reader there is a different bus, and reaching the terminus you'll find a sign saying 'Today'.

Be well, wherever you are, right now.

— ALESSANDRO MANZETTI, BRAM STOKER AWARD WINNER

CHAPTER ONE

IN THE DARK

WHEN THE NIGHT OWL SCREAMS

NEVER AGAIN WILL I VENTURE FAR

From my humble abode on a mid-winter eve

When night's lipless mouth has swallowed the sun

And its black sticky spit drools like rain

And the stars like multi-faceted eyes

Followed me through a tree-shrouded park

And grasped at me like weary claws

As I grew panicked and soon was lost

In this middling town I had known so well

Far from the oceans and the lakes

A full day's walk from any farm

And my sense of time grew awkward

For what might have been an hour or two or three

As dark, oily clouds blotted out the moon

I stumbled in widening circles

Wet gusts moving me Widdershins

Stinging my eyes, and face, and hands

And whispers called out to me

From behind every tree and bush

Telling me to lay down, and give up

And embrace the long, slow sleep,

And yes, I almost chose to release my sanity

But for an unearthly shriek and explosion of wings

That struck my shoulder blades like a fist

Driving me stumbling toward an odd distant light

Which soon became a street lamp

On a road I knew, which led back to my home.

Beware the night on all mid-winter eves

Because what's familiar is not all it seems

And pray you're pulled from the brink

when the night owl screams, when the night owl screams.

I DREAMED

I DREAMED I DIED LAST NIGHT
but not in some fantastic way
like pushed from a skyscraper's heights
and gunned down in a parking lot
nor screaming in a falling plane
crushed in a car on my cell phone
bleeding on a battlefield
or choking on a chicken bone.

Within my dream I woke upon
the very bed I know so well
yet different in the strangest way
that I sat up in sluggish fright
and startled that I felt so weak
I croaked a strange and fearful cry
then stumbled through my bathroom door
to face two aged bloodshot eyes.

And in the mirror of my dreams
my dead Father stared back at me
but unlike horrid memory
he looked now gaunt and world weary

until I saw his eyes were blue
when past were always hazel green
and so I came to see this truth
that I was frail and elderly.

I panicked through my rooms, amazed
to see the change of many years
dark peeling paint upon the walls
and flaking rugs on splintered floors
dull paintings crowding every space
old photos framed on dusty shelves
and yet no sign I shared this home
with any but my very self.

Exhaustion struck me deep within
and staggering I found my bed
whose ancient springs protested me
reclining with a shallow breath
I felt my will escaping me
and closing burning tear filled eyes
accepted my own deepest fear
that old and all alone I'd die.

And then I woke yet once again
not elderly but middle-aged

and ran to look upon my face
to see blonde hair instead of white
gaunt cheeks replaced with healthy fat
and all my teeth where they should be
and eyes still filled with dull delight
a quarter century reprieve.

Now one day later here I cower
upon the portal of that dream
and shamelessly I pray and plead
and ask the darkness what it brings.
Will I arise that aged man
so filled with dread and loneliness
or granted magic amnesty
awake both loved and bounteous?

I Dreamed

The Dunes in The Mist

MY SOUL GOT LOST IN PROVINCETOWN
one recent summer on a walk,
enveloped in nature's pale gown,
wispy and textured like white chalk.

It happened in the early morn
as I slowly strolled 'midst the dunes,
the sunrise still strangely unborn,
my footprints looking like odd runes.

The sharp, distant scream of seagulls
warned me against straying further
in this realm of dithers and lulls,
seducing with salty murmur.

Then just before the chasm clutched
my spirit irresistibly,
a stray mosquito gently touched
and spurred my hope's motility.

My own hand's dull, unconscious slap
opened my eyes with bald surprise,
spurring me to avert this trap
and flee to waves and azure skies.

INSOMNIE D'UN POÈTE

DID YOU EVER WAKE LATE AT NIGHT
filled with the strangest foreboding
you'd lost fate's fundamental fight
and there were no songs left to write,

that all books and stories were penned
and every muse had died or fled,
and leaving no way to transcend
the madness deep inside your head,

and next you found your soul can't speak
and no more poems would be written
because life lost all its mystique
and your heart could not be smitten,

just laying there in the shadows,
waiting for sleep to bless your eyes,
you pray morning would soon disclose
secrets wisdom can't catalyze.

Say, have you ever felt this way
lost in the gleams of blinding dreams

like demons led your mind astray

so far away

so far away...

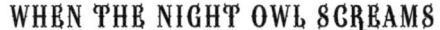

FEAR

FEAR, MY MOTHER FEAR, MY MATERNAL
Governess
You hold me tight within the darkness
Too long shielded from all harm
A babe in the wilderness.

Fear, my Father fear, my paternal General
You thrust me onto fields of battle
And cheer me like a Roman
And laugh at my Pyrrhic fall.

Fear, my Sister fear, my sororal Soul
You speak to me of journeys and The Call
And long nights of holy doubt
And see my faith's bitter toll.

Fear, my Brother fear, my fraternal Intellect
You open all the books didactic
And show me paths of wisdom
And find me less than logic.

Fear, my Lover fear, oh my sweet erosal Mate

You share my beds of failure

And you dance inside my hate

You sup upon my native Hells

And sing to me of wraiths

And you alone of all my weirds

Take pleasure in my mortal fate.

ANOTHER NIGHT

ANOTHER NIGHT SHE'S ALL ALONE
with just a glass of Malbec wine,
remembering his spiced cologne
reminiscent of moss and pine.

Another evening by herself,
sipping sweet spirits in shadow,
contemplating her long bookshelf
and framed photos of smiles that glow.

Another midnight harkening
to her soul's wearisome whispers
that lead to her hopes darkening,
missing the rub of his whiskers.

His death occurred at fate's fey whim
no fault of his, his absence is
an ache she still can't forgive him.

MOTHER DAEMON

SHE IS THE MOTHER OF DAEMONS
sowing eldritch legions,
she is the widow of chieftains
and the blight of seasons.

She rules not far beneath the earth,
eating moonlight and rain,
nature's only true virgin birth
and dreams are her domain.

She suckles mankind's every joy
with the milk of reason,
dangling it like a precious toy
and forbidden treason.

Her dark, maternal fingers play
across the breast of every day.

MOTHER DAEMON

ACCUSTOMED TO THE NIGHT

S HE IS ACCUSTOMED TO THE NIGHT,
its ebon drapery
that elicits naughty delight,
elusive, vapory.

She wears it like a second skin,
a thin, shadowy veil
that paints her soul with secret sin
read by fingers like braille.

She bathes in the thickest darkness,
serenaded by stars
that sing a sable song of flesh
leaving beautiful scars.

She is familiar with the night
which frees her from her daily plight.

MOONSHADE

SHE WALKED RIGHT OUT INTO THE WOOD
and then was never seen again
was what I was told in childhood
about this house that we'd moved in.

A young bride widowed much too soon
as her husband fell in a war
and during a lonely full moon
she left this world forevermore.

Her body was not ever found,
no marked gravestone to remember,
but when the full moon came around
I'd wake and see her pale specter.

I saw her walk across the glade
shoulders slumping her head drooping
fading into the tree's moonshade.

PENUMBRA BECKONS

HER SHADOW HAUNTS HIS WAKING
dreams
with soft and enticing contours
flowing from eternity's seams
with smile that beguiles and allures.

Her shade appears by summoning
all of the amber joy inside
which he can find by humbling
his own pretentious, painful pride.

Her relief is carved by the sun,
displayed in loving perfection,
a guest who will not ever shun
or reject his sweet attention.

A phantom beautiful and rare
a silhouette and charmed coquette
most comely lass with ebon hair.

WHEN THE NIGHT OWLS SING

I DREAM OF WHEN THE NIGHT OWLS SING
with wide swept wings 'pon ebon wind
and moon wolves sweetly howling
and tears of rain on nature's chin.

I see owls soaring beneath stars,
dancing above forest fingers,
oblivious to all time's scars
in realms where amity lingers.

They cloister in bewitching choirs
on green branches with fuchsia leaves,
sad eyes reflecting finite fires
of all the sins that mankind breeds.

My soul they now illuminate
until morning when I must wake.

DARK BLOSSOM

S HE BLINDS HERSELF TO SUFFERING
witnessed throughout a painful life
and memories of plundering
and all manner of sorry strife.

She spurns the light of any hope
and promises of better days
as both too often just elope
before consummation assays.

Not heeding dire dejection's smile,
immune to fear's distracting wink,
ignoring all that's vain and vile,
now free of disappointment's stink.

She dodders in divine darkness
the bloom of horror's harsh harvest.

TEARS OF THE MOON

WALKING ALONE BEYOND DUSK,
cloaked in dark, moist garments of night,
I breathe deeply of summer musk
and smile at nature's hidden virtuosos
filling the thick, sweet air with music.
Silent, ebony skins of water
ripple gently with silver tears
falling from her sad, haunting eye.

DOWN IN THE DARK REALMS

ANOTHER DAY COMES TO ITS END
whence I can retreat into sleep
and my spirit will thus descend
down to dark realms wondrous and deep

with horizons that never stop
and odd, green and lavender skies
and stars that never dance or drop
and oceans filled with tickling sighs.

I stand upon a solid shore
as warm, red waters bathe my feet
and crashing waves sing out a roar
filling me until I'm complete.

Street Specter

YOU'VE SEEN HIM IN SO MANY TOWNS,
reflected on the wettest roads
in windows while making his rounds
within the shade of all life's foes.

He's never given twice a look,
barely rippling in memory,
neither a hero nor a crook,
yet both familiar and scary.

His aspect hidden in shadow,
his desire in concrete and steel,
his soul as ancient as sorrow,
his heart every city's keel.

He is the specter of the streets
the grime and grit driving spirit
that rises above all defeats.

BEWARE

BEWARE THE TOUCH OF SULTRY EYES
that fain appear like bright sunrise,
surprising and mesmerizing
the unwary with their charmed guise.

Beware the ode that these looks sing,
the siren call that takes to wing
and lifts your soul to fly with it,
a gaze both knowing and glowing.

Beware the hunger in this stare
that aches to taste your every care,
to feast upon your helplessness
as your heart melts within its glare.

Such sweet creatures will have their way
conquering men time and again
with beauty pure, eldritch, and fey.

EMERGING

SHE IS EMERGING FROM SHADOWS
under the brushstroke of moonlight,
a bouquet of blooming mallows
born in the auspices of night.

She is poised between darkest dark
and a milky, luminous light,
a harlequin dressed in the spark
of spells cast by a willful sprite.

A moment that just cannot end,
a strange, wondrous dichotomy,
two raw extremes that will not blend,
a calm, conflicting symphony.

When fully hatched, what will she be
war-torn aesthete at last complete
courting chaos or harmony.

MISTER DEADSMILE

O N AN APRIL NIGHT WHEN THE AIR IS
cold,
when the wolves all sleep and shadows are bold,
when the moon never blinks its yellow eye
the wise ones say Mister Deadsmile is nigh.

He's waiting at the end of winding roads
looking for sinners to suffer his woes
like those who do wrong then run from their homes
heedless of fate and the horror it bodes.

That which confines him is compelled to free
this specter that malefactors can't flee,
baleful apparition tasting the breeze
and licking the scent of every sin's flea.

His grin as wide as a shark-filled shoreline
with eyes as black as a cadaver's brine,
his laughter an icy and shocking cry,
his touch, oh his touch, will chill and malign.

So think twice my children before you act,

committing transgressions, breaking the pact
then blindly flying until you are trapped
for Deadsmile is fingering your contract.

THE ASTRONAUT NIGHTMARE

AGAIN THE ASTRONAUT NIGHTMARE
invades my deepest darkest sleep,
stripping my sense of whimsy bare,
exposing the sky's savage sweep.

I'm dropping up into the black,
plummeting toward pale silver stars
without the aid of a jet-pack
or rocket ship or flying cars.

Powerless against this strange pull
as if the heavens tethered me
like an eldritch umbilical
leashing soul with eternity.

Helpless I'm falling off the Earth
over gravity's shadowed ledge,
a weightless horrifying birth
plunging up towards an endless depth.

BOATMAN TARRY NOUGHT

OH DISTANT BOATMAN TARRY NOUGHT
as I am ready for this quest,
my flesh is weak and brow is hot
and I long for infinite rest.

Kind boatman I beg you make haste
to the shores of my failing soul
and rescue me from this pale waste
as I wade into doom's dark shoal.

Fair boatman I call out to you
and sing life's most honest lament
that I'll pay mercy's revenue
with the coins placed on my eye's flesh.

Oh how I yearn and long to be
gloriously on death's journey
'pon the seas of eternity.

SOULBEARERS

CAN YOU HEAR THE MOURNFUL LAMENT
    accompanying soulbearers
echoing that all hope is spent
after this dark reign of terrors.

They shuffle slowly toward the light,
a distant promise most can't see
through shadowed hallways of a blight
destroying all complacency.

Their burden is a loathsome lot,
conveying what was once precious
souls cut down by unfair onslaught,
left frightened, bleeding, then breathless.

This twilight walk is all too long
and their burden a penitence
but one they'll embrace 'til the dawn
of mankind's nascent righteousness.

GATHER

GATHERING PLACE OF EXPELLED SOULS
are you, perhaps, growing too fast,
filling with the unfinished scrolls
of lives that have too quickly passed.

Strange twilight realm of shock and grief
your traffic has greatly increased
and like a tree stripped of each leaf
I think Earth feeds you a raw feast.

There are too many traveling
across this once sublime expanse,
their radiance unraveling
off of the spool of life's dire dance.

A dark uncalled for unity
born of hate's vile impunity.

THE NIGHT FLOODS OF HEBEI

I JUST HEARD ABOUT CHINA'S FLOOD
swarming the people late at night,
disaster no one understood
that struck with a horrific bite.

It came when all were fast asleep
long after dusk had said goodnight,
a terror leaving most to weep
thousands of homes lost in this plight.

Nearly two hundred have just died
and hundreds more are missing still
as the shameless receding tide
slowly reveals the reaper's bill.

I know this dark assassin waits
so violent and yet silent,
mercurial it vacillates,
planning sins it will not repent.

CHAPTER TWO

OTHERWORLDLY

SATURN'S STAIN

SOMETHING STRANGE HAPPENED TO
Saturn,
they say it has changed its colors
all across the north pole's border
where the fiercest vortex shudders.

In twenty twelve it was blue-black
and now it is the brightest gold
as if a skin of old shellac
flaked off revealing life below.

In the same intervening years
my own soul did the opposite
where once was joy and amber cheers
has now been stained by fortune's spit.

Perhaps a cosmic irony
or some haunting disharmony
connects this dark giant and me
damning my pale complacency.

SATURN'S STAIN

ATHENA STRUCK

IT DIED WHILE FLYING STRAIGHT AT HER,
striking, full-force, the farmhouse wall
directly behind her shoulder
she felt the death of spotted owl.

She looked outside and found its form
upon some weeds and colored leaves,
perhaps an omen for a storm
beyond everything she perceives.

There was no window between them,
so how could this raptor have known,
why would it even give a damn
that she sat sad and all alone.

She contemplates the hoary price
of this unnerving sacrifice.

THE SCARY BAZAAR

EACH NIGHT I ENTER THE SCARY BAZAAR
to shop for vile thoughts macabre and bizarre,
salty frights for a hungry audience
and at least three boxes of naughtiness.

I squint and smile at fellow consumers
all scrambling for hauntings, hates, and tumors,
wary of sunrise and a deadline's knell,
jealously guarding their own gathered hell.

At the checkout counter my bill's rung up,
nightmares, bad memories, a blood-filled cup,
gory descriptions, cultural taboos
and self-loathing rantings fueled by booze.

I walk these dark goods back to my abode
and prepare to cook a horrific ode.

TRACKER

S HE HUNTS FOR ME, I KNOW SHE DOES,
this lovely fiend from colder climes,
wolf skin clad land of savages
teeming with dark portents and signs.

Cloaked in elaborate headdress
that decorates her fierce, fey face,
this harsh, unrelenting huntress
is filled with strength and fleet of pace.

I sense her behind every tree
along the highways that I drive
and no matter how fast I flee
I fear she'll soon be by my side.

She wants to feel my beating heart
pressing against her swelling breast,
refusing to let me depart
after the kiss that spurned her quest.

Her hunger is insatiable
and won't subsist until a tryst
leaves her soul both sated and full.

LOVE LETTER TO THE ABYSS

SHRUGGING INTO MY CHEAP RAIN COAT
purchased at a corner drug store
I wear it like an arcane shroud
as I stumble out my front door
greeting a morning black and wet
muffled by raindrops striking me
with an otherworld harmony
and strangely twilight melody
I tread this pavement like a dream
immune to bark, horn, and sidewalk
commuting through purgatory
'til street light and curb make me balk.
Now sable puddle mirrors me
in shades of sweet melancholy
pure sheet of glistening ebony
reflecting sublime tragedy.

It offers dark necrotic bliss
an end to pain and all life's rain
as I dive into the abyss.

TRAIN TRACKS

I THINK THAT I HAVE FOUND THE TRUTH,
the answer to our darkest fear,
the steam trumpet that gives warning,
a way to know when death draws near,
for passing now through middle age
I found myself soon noticing
the odd abandoned railroad tracks
nearby before disappearing.
These sights increase numerically
as I now slowly realize
as my blonde hair turns silvery
I see the rails that death must ride,
traveling to friends, commuting work,
beyond the streets, among the trees
this path the reaper must traverse
over mossy, rotting bridges
or fields that mark the end of hurts.

On long lost locomotive roads
I hear my death's dark chariot
a ghost train's whistle that forebodes.

In The Greys, The Pale, The Gloom

I AM LOST OUT HERE IN THE GREYS,
stumbling from one stain to the next,
pushing my way through a dense haze
vexing me like a warlock's hex.

I am far astray in the pale,
beyond the borders of safety,
worse than the darkest fairy tale,
within a furlong of crazy.

I am vanishing in the gloom
and I fight it every day,
retracing my footsteps of doom
on strange paths that led me astray.

Though listless and cloaked in despair
still pushing on toward distant dawn
I drag my feet and whisper prayer.

SPIRIT PHOTOGRAPHY

SHE DOES NOT KNOW WHAT OTHERS SEE
beneath her shell of breath and flesh
captured spirit photography
showing how skin and soul enmesh.

It is a most graceful haunting,
an amber ghost inside of her
enchanting as it is daunting,
this chamber of pleasure and hurt.

A still life of a mortal frame,
an after-image of a life,
a virile and vermillion flame,
a song from her heart's drum and fife.

This doorway to an inner light
fate's raw tincture paints a picture
portrait of a candle at night.

DID YOU EVER

DID YOU EVER FEEL LIKE A DOLL
owned by some uncaring godlings
who like to laugh as you just fall
with faulty toy parachute strings
that snap and break as you tumble
into some grey, decayed dollhouse,
left to slowly peel and crumble
as like adults they wine and grouse,
tossing lightning bolts and thunder,
striking the shores with tsunami,
allowing sickness to plunder
and bloody wars the weak can't flee.

Don't you think that one almighty
should act more grown up, just maybe?

LEGEND OF THE CICERO SWAMP DOG

SOME CALL THE SWAMP DOG A TALL TALE,
a story to frighten the kids,
a warning to children who fail
to clean their rooms, or tell big fibs.

The swamp dog prowls in big back yards,
a wet and motley rough-born pooch
sung of round fires by ancient bards,
a beast whose temperament is huge.

With muddy paws and wet whiskers
and a ferocious fearsome mug,
this swamp-bred brute growls and whispers
he'll jump bad boys who act too smug.

So after dusk beware tree lines
don't dip your toes in Cicero's
inhabited and clammy climes.

FLIODHAIS

AN IRISH TOUR GUIDE ONCE TOLD ME
a scarred stone effigy still stands,
a visage from eternity,
a raw beauty still echoing
aspects of sylvan harmony,
a work worshiped with loving craft
by sculptor's hands and believers,
a forest goddess from the past.
Then this Celtic lass said with pride,
"Fliodhais, empress of truth seekers
and every tree's bucolic bride!"

Now wraith and wandering widow
since Eire was stripped of all oak-kind
where ghostly leaves weep and billow.

AUTOMATON

MY RADIANT AUTOMATON,
you just incorporated me
like an emotionless Don Juan
made of tempting machinery.

Your perfection is astounding,
a lovely, flawless work of art,
a mechanistic fey foundling
that so slyly lock-picked my heart.

But there ends equanimity
as you merely reciprocate
my love with simple mimicry,
feelings you only imitate.

The beauty molded on your shell
empty inside a hollow bride
and structure where love cannot dwell.

BLACK AND WHITE

I'M TRAPPED IN A BLACK AND WHITE WORLD
and living a black and white life
where all my pigments have unfurled,
migrating where bonheur is rife.

I move through black and white panels
that frame my labored lack of choice
like fading black and white candles
burning all the hopes most rejoice.

I see through black and white glasses
offering denatured visions
of rainbows turning to ashes
for my black and white decisions.

Beware doorways to black and white
their passage is a damning blight.

COUPLES COUNSELING

JUST YESTERDAY MORNING, FIFTY YEARS ago

a widower mourned for his laughing widow

while covered in moonlight deep underground

they both sang and screamed without any sound

skating on jello and tuning a tree,

lost in a graveyard afloat on the sea.

LIVING ASLEEP

I'VE BEEN LIVING ASLEEP, AND CAN'T WAKE
up,
just drifting through my life with my eyes closed,
trying to drink from a bottomless cup,
traveling 'tween dreams and nightmare transposed.

I stumble through mists of grasping people,
insubstantial fingers slipping through me
like I'm trapped inside a cathedral
where creatures of light worship falsity.

My mystic craft beaches on shores of snores,
beams and bulkheads bound by desperation,
eroded by dark slumbering sea-swords
striking at me as I search for haven.

My heart has been lethargic and drowsy
as my soul screams for release quite loudly.

A LOVERS' TALE

IT IS LATE IN THE MONTH OF NOVEMBER
when maple trees, sleeping, no longer bleed;
and my night hike grows sullen and sober;
my heart feels a chill mysterious need.

Thus I wrestle and fight with the mountain
so swift in reckless and savage ascent
that I soon find a warm breathing fountain
draining from crimson and soft pulsing vents.

Bathing my worries and cleansing my fears
at peace like a child afloat in the womb.
Calliope whispers, "I'll join you dear."
Specters of love 'neath a still sapphire moon.

In time my eyes spot a phantom --
a shadowed strange plot of earth newly raised;
and so stepping up out of the fountain
I walk mesmerized with unblinking gaze.

And thus shaking I see the gray marker;
trembling and deaf to Calliope's wails;

and I know as the moon becomes darker
that something's amiss, and beyond the pale.

So I read the harsh blackened inscription
which burrows down to the roots of my soul --
unjust prey of an awful affliction;
my shy love who left me three years ago.

And now gasping I wake feeling smothered.
Shaking and sweating I crawl from my bed
and I whimper and cry for my lover
this dream which my heart has unnaturally wed.

Thus for years I have dared my reflection
courage to journey this terrible way.
Now I sever life's tender affection
and guilt, and sorrow, and shame bleach away.

I will enter the realm of the mountain
to join Calliope's wandering soul;
and we'll swim and we'll live by the fountain
whose clear gentle waters eternally flow.

And my vision becomes ever clearer
and fiery demons stop clawing my chest;

and with her warm sweet lips drawing nearer
I know that my spirit can finally rest.

AT STOKERCON

WHERE FARES THE LITERARY SPAWN
of all that's dark and full of dread,
to StokerCon to StokerCon where fun is cut and joy is
bled.

To StokerCon to StokerCon
they sang on train, and car, and plane,
a hair-raising and chilling song,
a dirge foreboding weekend's bane.

So now they drink, and laugh, and dance,
these ghoulish authors of terror
proposing a gothic advance
like sanity's pale pall-bearer.

They're stalking stalls and haunting halls,
reading aloud their creepy tomes
between StokerCon's ghastly walls
rumored to hide James Herbert's bones.

What will they raise by Monday's dawn
at StokerCon, at StokerCon,

what evil wraith of fetid faith,

perhaps Bael or Thoth-Amon.

TEARS

THE TEARS OF CHILDREN HURT THE MOST,
they well from primal pain and fear,
from rivers of dark unseen ghosts
that always threaten to appear.

The tears of mothers are treasures,
gold coins in chests of raw worry
paying the cost of those pleasures
granted as life's divine dowry.

The tears of angels are the worst,
their pity is contemptuous
with sorrows that can't quench the thirst
of those who never tasted bliss.

Each tear is one drop in a sea
a reservoir and pale memoir
of all that innocence can't flee.

AFTERNOON CHESS WITH SMOKE AND BLOOD

THREE LOVELY LADIES PLAYING CHESS
before the autumn wind turns chill,
luxuriating in the press
of fallen leaf and shed bird quill,
sipping blood tea with grand noblesse
against the foot of grief's dark hill
laughing at pawns in dire distress
and armies slain in Fall's sweet spill.

HEAT DOME

THEY SAY THAT THERE IS A HEAT DOME,
a frightening, dreadful construct,
the dark nightmare of nature's gloom
released because of our conduct.

Perhaps it is a new judgment,
a punishment for mankinds' crime,
a hot and blistering torment
appearing as this burning sign.

Or worse it is our own sick child
born of Earth's fiery, scalding sin
and all the passions we have riled
this summer of hate's ascension.

Searing monster of no surprise
to those of us who cut it's ties.

STRANGER THINGS

ONE NIGHT I CHANCED 'PON STRANGER
Things,
a dark and mesmerizing tale
of all the carnage science brings
and one child abducted by hell.

Spellbound with a burgeoning dread
of a mother who lost her son,
three boys each one a staunch brave friend
and an eldritch girl on the run.

Enticed with spicy mystery
and frightening astral projections,
membraneous and silvery
portal bridging dimensions.

Love triangle of teenagers,
bullies both mean and threatening,
weird monster with teeth like razors
and one Sheriff's dead reckoning.

No one is safe to walk alone

in Hawkins' shadowy forest
when upside-down ghouls stalk and roam
in search of blood and human flesh.

Macabre mayhem and stranger things
ebullient, swishing, silent
ooze from the Duffer brothers' dreams.

In The Mirror

S HE WAS CAPTURED BY THE MIRROR,
right in the middle of a pause
when the moment chose to glimmer
and she was taken without cause.

She was frozen in reflection,
so proudly posed both lithe and taut,
forming a raw, ripe connection
within a realm devoid of thought.

She was tricked by the looking glass
and oh so quickly mesmerized,
seduced by shining frames of brass
claiming a beauty it has prized.

Like stars that wither in the dawn
her mortal flesh has travelled on.

THE PROJECTIONIST'S POEM

I AM SURROUNDED BY DEAD MEN
wishing that I was one of them,
a thing without weight or substance,
a framed flicker and whiskered whim.

Sometimes they all beckon to me,
shallow shades of frivolity
mocking my solitary trade
with their cold celluloid esprit.

I know that they no longer breathe
and have no truths left to bequeath,
pimping forged immortality
like fake vampires with fanged false teeth.

Projected on my soul's pale screen
the mark of a film grave robber,
a vicarious libertine
and sad late show Necromancer.

YESTERDAY'S SNOW

WHAT HAPPENED TO YESTERDAY'S SNOW
and why did it decide to go
so early in this cold season
when sledders snarl and glaciers glow.

What happened to the day before
when pale blankets lay at my door
as if moonlight had come to life
and spread its pelt across earth's floor.

What happened to the frosty nights
and spirits sipped by northern lights
and kissing near a fireplace
while soaking in Winter's delights.

Where it has gone I do not know,
perhaps to that mythic white crow
who flies always above the clouds
seeking fate's fickle black rainbow.

POSSESSED

THE INTERNET IS CALLING HER,
enticing and enthralling her,
mesmerizing her very soul
with prurience, and shock, and slur.

The world wide web is spelling her,
concerning and compelling her
to stimulate her humble heart,
jabbing with a saccadic spur.

The networks are all vexing her,
handicapping and hexing her,
charming and bewitching her mind
with visions she cannot deter.

Yes horrified and yet beguiled
she drinks a mix of this vile fix
whose taste is never reconciled.

Chapter Three

Confessions

SOWING

I THINK, IN TIME, ALL POETS SEE
the buds of that potential truth
that years of penning poetry
gives birth to an undying tooth,

cuspid, canine, fang if you will,
a hard and home-grown appendage
allowing the unholy thrill
of biting through deceit's bandage,

chewing into the falsities
people apply to memories
to heal history's pedigrees
of our daily atrocities.

We bastard bards and elegists
sow sacred seeds like Delphic deeds
casting candor from rhyming fists.

DRIVING HOME FROM RAVENCON

MOVING THROUGH BURNT SIENNA
valleys of spring drought,
Virginia, Maryland, Delaware, New Jersey,
beneath a distant amber sun and cold blue sky
nature's mane is brittle upon these asphalt shoulders
shedding a scaly scurf of big rig shredded tires
sprinkled like black licorice on cement fondant
and I ponder this dearth within my sour soul
and the trail of iridescent, tasteless bread crumbs
that like this narrowing, straight highway have led to
a twilight life of literary ambitions,
day dreams, and all too rare human interaction
that by its nature is an unnerving maelstrom
of extroverted smiles, cosplay enthusiasts
and the imaginative camaraderie of
honeyed spirits and winter wine at midnight hour
that dares, so haughtily dares to drag me kicking
and screaming out of this imposed lethargy that
has trapped me, and pulled me down, a psychic
   quicksand

of unhappy doubts and loneliness, straight jacket
of alluring melancholy that my veins now spit
out, shed and drain away as crippling addiction.

For Food And Boots

RTISTS, MUSICIANS, AND POETS,
some say we are all prostitutes
among entertainment's lowest,
selling our souls for food and boots.

Singers and sculptors and dancers
honing fine skills across the years,
becoming culture's grandmasters
yet targeted by shameless jeers.

Uncivil voices of dissent,
pranksters and howlers from the mobs,
petty, faceless phantoms that vent
self-loathing pointing out false flaws.

Perhaps the true measure of art
is not grand praise nor cheers we raise
but all the blades aimed at our heart.

DRUNKEN SOCIOLOGIST IN SOHO BAR

THE EDUCATED MIDDLE CLASS,
not all, but those who love to preach,
each one a vile and pompous ass
who has nothing but bile to teach.

Lording their humble beginnings
like a scepter that knighted fools,
baptizing their too worthy souls
and blessing all their lofty goals.

None ambitious as the Bourgeois,
none as arrogant or as flawed,
bleating decrees of common law
like a lion-tamer just clawed.

Their advice does naught but condemn
oh what a crime I'm one of them!

From Midnight's Keep

SHE CALLS TO ME FROM SOMEWHERE near,
some quiet place I cannot hear
singing a whisper so gently
it barely tickles my pale ear.
She calls to me when I'm asleep,
when snuggling snores and murmurs creep,
chanting to me from midnight's keep
upon the willowy wind's sweep.
She calls to me, demure siren
from shores both lonely and barren,
enticing with a tepid tone
smooth as an ancient polished stone.
Perhaps she's born of secret scrolls
and silent dreams that touch men's souls
with dark magics no mortal knows
beyond the power of mere prose
where all eternity now glows
with the gravity of rainbows.

Reflected Me

PLAINLY FOR ANYONE TO SEE
two different mirrored sides of me,
one oft on edge and one at ease
yet both share the same pedigree.
Captured in a silver echo,
each one a familiar fellow,
both momentary phantasms
as thoughtful as they are shallow.
One fears each ever-changing day
at odds with time's endless decay,
one contemplates eternal stars
and welcomes every pathway.
Yet everyday that I wake up
I don't know who will come to be,
which one will fill my coffee cup
and whose soul has reflected me.

MY EVERY CELL

FOR MY SURVIVORS IF MY AIRPLANE
crashed
on this trip I am reluctant to take
and this long aluminum shell just smashed
into mountains for my pilot's mistake.

This accident has caught me by surprise,
I did not write a poem for my own wake
and unlike Lucifer's fall from bright skies
I will not rise from a fiery lake.

Know that my whole life did not flood my mind
before my death as my memory sucks
and neither did my innermost soul find
sweet Nirvana when my flesh became flux.

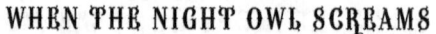

DREAD

IT'S FOUR O'CLOCK, AM THAT IS,
you know, the time some farmers wake
before the sun slowly rises
when bread and donuts start to bake.

It's four o'clock and all is still,
commuters have not started cars,
some conquered by a sleeping pill,
others passed out from hopping bars.

It's four o'clock and pretty dark,
the moon has not yet come this way,
when lazy dogs refuse to bark
at passing squirrels or mice at play.

It's four o'clock and you don't know
what startled you right out of sleep,
maybe a whisper from a crow
or worse a shout from somewhere deep.

It's four o'clock and you're sweating,
knowing truth is just out of reach,

struggling against this bloodletting

by guilt's dark, existential leech.

CHAPTER FOUR

GHOSTS OF THE PAST

DUCK!

I T WASN'T AN AQUATIC BIRD
that we all feared would soon appear
but a piercing siren just heard
that filled us with sickening fear.

Then a couple of years later
when we were bigger boy or girl,
though doomed to fry in a crater,
hugged walls as hell braced to unfurl.

And later yet, young teenagers,
we're told the Junior High cellars
would bunker a few from dangers
with most left outside like beggars.

Looking back now I cannot say
of all that dread of death's hot tread
if it was real or shadow-play.

WHEN LUGGAGE HAD NO WHEELS

REMEMBER WHEN SUITCASES HAD NO wheels
or titanium legs and arms
and they were not charged like electric eels
to fry any causes of harms?

Remember when cars couldn't drive alone
and never had an argument
and would never beg in a monotone
you plow tailgaters in cement?

Remember when the airport had no scans
and did not probe your veins and bone
or wrap your chest in paralysis bands
in case you're a terrorist clone?

Before air filters were put in our lungs
Before most of the ocean died
Before icebergs melted and flooded shores
Before the world woke up and cried.

WE WERE WHIPPED

YES, WE WERE WHIPPED WHEN WE WERE
bad,
he used a long black leather belt,
stripped 'til our buttocks were not clad,
judged worthy of many a welt.

The crimes were few but serious,
using a car like a playground,
pushing a sibling in a brook,
playing with matches we had found.

All of this by the age of ten,
now I've lived over fifty years,
I have not fathered anyone,
and oft ponder those ancient tears.

That warped confusion of childhood
harsh discipline greeting each sin
life lessons learning bad from good.

THE ANCIENT LANGUAGE OF FINGERS

THERE IS A GENERATION GAP BETWEEN
children of today with their brawny texting-thumbs
and we archaic ribbon jockeys of yesteryear,
we graduates of business typing boot camp,
that harsh basic training taken in high school
the senior year that my hands were paired with
months of hardship, field-stripping key functions,
the standard QWERTY meme
hard wired into a decade of acolytes
inheriting microchip keyboards in our twenties,
stabbing them with calloused fingers blooded for
battle on frightening standard typewriters,
brutal machines cobbled from stamped steel parts,
filling the newly born mac and PC micro-clusters
with the angry computer punk-music
and heavy staccato of eighty plus WPM.

CANNONEER

UPON THIS BED I PLEAD MY CASE
with sad regard and aged breath,
old powder scars upon my face,
this Cannoneer now faces death.

Deserving not my mortal wrath
and Shaitan's urge to rend and kill,
the unwise souls who crossed my path
did pay the bloody butcher's bill.

'Gainst many forts in distant lands
I unleashed thunder on war's slaves
As lightning from my leathered hands
Toppled walls and slaughtered knaves.

Among the waves of Mother Sea
I shot my ball and great ships sank
and with a fey and evil glee
I fed the Ocean gore and plank.

Then soon my name would thus portend
a most unholy bloody fuss,

A reputation that I tend,
Mars' terrible own blunderbuss.

In time I earned a Sergeant's stripe
and healthy fat upon my shank,
until my punishment grew ripe,
and fate attacked my wretched flank.

A freckled lad untried and scared
Overpacked my cannon's bore
And as the touch-hole belched and flared
I felt the iron fist of Thor.

Screaming beneath a medic's saw,
a legless pension for this fiend,
Four decades now my sorrow raw,
for all mortals I cannon-cleaved.

My feeble eyes grow faint and dim,
The rumble of artillery near,
"Descend Cur!" Quoth the Reaper's din,
"For final judgement, Cannoneer!"

CANNONEER

NOTHING EVER CHANGES

FOR SEVENTEEN YEARS I HAVE LIVED
in this garden apartment complex
in the same one bedroom apartment
upon the same hardwood floors
surrounded by the same walls
that wear the same eggshell-hued clothes,
drinking water from the same chrome faucet
and every year has four seasons
and I see the world from the same vantages,
watching snow fall from the front windows,
viewing fireworks through the back door,
spying on my parked car from my bedroom,
hearing the ice cream truck play its song,
listening to the screams and laughter of children,
finding the same junk-mail in my postbox,
seeing the same Asian woman
performing Tai Chi in the front courtyard
and never having the courage
to approach her and say hello
and tell her that I once studied
Mandarin Chinese in the U.S. Air Force

well over thirty years ago…

Nothing ever changes… ever.

At The Carnival

SHE'S AT THE CARNIVAL AGAIN,
at least that's what she tells her soul
each day that she chooses to feign
delight wherever she may stroll.

By sheer willpower and desire
she fabricates a wonderland
out of society's dark mire
and rampant sins always at hand.
She nimbly sidesteps pushy clowns
and laughs back at the barker's calls,
dancing to this midway's crass sounds
while winking at the kewpie dolls.
Framed by her unseen spectacles,
each lens a magic looking glass
offering up false miracles
traded for life's maudlin morass.
Refusing to accept the truth
she lets her smile just drift awhile
indulging her spirit's sweet tooth.

THE GOSSAMER GHOSTS
OF RAINBOW RUN

THE GOSSAMER GHOSTS OF RAINBOW RUN,
I've seen them dance, fleeing the sun
like some wondrous fable of youth
across my farm's far horizon.

They only come at dawn and dusk,
fearful of high noon's mighty light,
yet neither do they grant their trust
to all the stars and moon at night.

A garish and romantic lot,
these gypsies of errant mirage,
too fast to let themselves be caught
hiding in nature's camouflage.

Vivid pigments, they form a weave
binding the vale of rainbow run
wearing a forest as each sleeve
and river slacks that god has spun.

Each passing year fewer have come,

less for feeble eyes to undress

as I ponder the sad autumn

of their long fading radiance.

Chapter Five

Archaeology of Flesh

FIRE

WHILE WALKING OUTSIDE NOT TOO
long ago
I smelled a rancid pungent odor.
The burning scent of something synthetic.
And my nose wrinkled and I coughed
and soon enough it wafted away from me.
But for some reason I could not shake it.
And so this strange unsettling shadow
followed me into the deepest sleep of all.

And so I dreamed,
but a dream,
unlike any other.
For in this dream I traveled back,
far back.
Into my past.
My forgotten past.
The archive of my soul.
Back to when I was a boy.
A time I no longer knew.
Back to when I was an Army brat.
One of five.

And my father was a Sergeant in the military.
And we lived in the Perlacher Forest Army Housing
    Project
in Munich, Germany.

It was 1969 .
And it was late in the year.
And winter was on its way.
And I was not a very bright child,
at nearly seven years of age,
for I was repeating the first grade.
And we lived in a three-bedroom two-bathroom
    apartment.
On the third floor of a three-floor building.
On-base housing.

And for the past week I had been writing to Santa Claus.
Sharing the Sears and Roebuck catalog with my siblings.
Filling letters with lists of toys that I wanted for
    Christmas.
GI Joe dolls,
with many outfits,
and accessories.
And all manner of air-rifles,
and toy machine guns,

and cap pistols,

that I could use when playing "Army," outside, with my
    brothers,

filling the surrounding neighborhood with our savage
    yells of

"You'd dead!" and "I killed you!" and "No you didn't!"

And in school the spirit of the holidays was everywhere

and our homeroom teacher taught us to cut paper angels

and create elaborate snowflakes with a single sheet of
    paper

and make our own greeting cards to show our parents.

And though my birthday was still a week and a half away

I kept reminding my mother that she had to make the
    cupcakes,

the 30 chocolate cupcakes I would bring to my
    homeroom,

on my seventh birthday,

just like several of my classmates had already done this
    year.

And then,

on a cold cloudy day this mid-December

we had all come dressed in our good clothes to school

for today we had our little Christmas celebration

and we all sat behind our desks with smiles on our faces

and our teacher,

Ms. Mueller,

handed out white candles to all.

And then she lit all the candles

which stood in the middle of our desks.

And then she closed the blinds and turned out the lights.

And then we all started singing

"Silent Night, Holy Night."

And it was like a sweet shroud of magic had settled upon
   us.

And then there was a piercing squeal.

And the horror started.

And there was a flash of yellow light to my right.

Brighter than all the candles combined.

And a weird "whooshing" sound.

And a warm burst of air hit my right side.

And a horrid awful chemical smell filled my nostrils in
   the semi-darkness.

And then the overhead lights suddenly came on.

And Ms. Mueller flew across the front of the room,

a green army blanket in her arms.

And she thrust the blanket upon my classmate Susan,

whose head of thick fluffy brown curls had turned into a
    flaming torch
and she was screaming,
and burning,
and writhing in the smoking remains of the diaphanous
    light-blue princess dress
she had worn to school that day.

And then I awoke,
in a dramatic Hollywood pool of sweat,
and realizing this was not a dream.
And I shivered,
and knew,
remembering,
the truth of it.
That I had managed to hide from for almost four decades,
accosting me now,
unforgivably,
in middle-age.
That awful smell.
That rancid nauseating unholy smell...

Lost Dogs Of The Finger Lakes

ALL MY LIFE I HAVE BATHED IN
loneliness
like a decadent, lethargic Roman
scrubbing the blood of violent conquest
off of my weathered, and stained, and scarred soul,
a cleansing and safe purification
separating me from scary masses
and all too jarring and tactile handshakes
and frank unnerving intimacies of
piercing face to face communication.
I have dried my naked dreams in towels
of indifference and wash cloths of fear,
allowing the light of isolation
so empowering and overwhelming
to knead and massage and comfort my heart,
an under-used and oft-neglected thing
that still aches to pump hope's formaldehyde
throughout my failing necrotic psyche
preserving this semblance of mortal life,
this jarred and pickled exhibit that pens

rudimentary and banal poems,

unfit for any human consumption,

the merest refuse of much grander meals

and the guttural mumblings of defeat...

THE MODERNIST PROMETHEUS

I F I HAD VINCENT VAN GOGH'S EAR
and Hellenic Homer's pale eye
would I hear nature's sweet veneer
and see the truth in every lie.

If I had ancient Aegles' voice
and Tycho Brahe's Danish nose
would I speak against unjust choice
and sense that starlight never froze.

If I had Francis Le Clerc's leg
or Gaius Scaevola's right hand
would I be more brazen in bed
and promptly defend righteous land.

Could an alchemist rebuild me
with every part that gives souls heart
free of weak flesh's slavery.

THE PATH

HE WALKS A STARK AND LONELY PATH
longer than he remembers why,
perhaps because the distant past
echoes a fading battle cry,

that sadly dissipates and wanes
not unlike a worn, ill-kept road
that twists and turns like ancient veins
threading the flesh of life's abode.

He carries all his fears and sins
in satchels wedded to his heart,
a weight felt from shoulders to shins
as his eyes gaze on welcome dirt.

Just one more mile, just one more hill
just one more step by force of will.

WE ALL BLEED

WE ALL BLEED IN DIFFERENT WAYS
from that moment when we are born
to the end of all of our days
we know just what it means to mourn.

We all bleed from the cuts and wounds
allotted us throughout our lives,
reaped from the blessings and the dooms
that threaten souls like unsheathed knives.

We all bleed from the inside out,
from damage hidden and unseen
that wells until it has to spout
in geysers scarlet and serene.

In each of us is a dark seed
a promised verse to bless or curse
that grows in everything we bleed.

WHAT DOES IT MEAN

WHAT DOES IT MEAN TO BE ALONE,
to roam a city like a ghost,
encircled by couples unknown
to loneliness's sharp riposte.

What does it mean, being a soul
standing in front of monuments,
ending a solitary stroll
with no one to share your comments.

What does it mean when surrounded
by thousands on a sunny day
and yet feel fate has thus pounded
your hopes to defeat's dark decay.

Perhaps every life has its pall
an equal mix of bad and bliss
not meaning anything at all.

FOUND

FOUND NOW BY ALL THAT I HAVE FLED
Found by everything I dread
Found out to be less than I've said
Found lacking inside my own head.

Found in the most secure hideout
Found by the most discerning eyes
Found without a mere sprout of doubt
Found in the shade of fibs and lies.

Found to be much more than you knew
Found not to be as pure as dew
Found in ways angels would eschew
Found without any ballyhoo.

Found in the clearest flat expanse
Found within reach of happenstance
Found not performing any dance
Found by neither mistake nor chance.

Found with my silent approval
Found by the bread crumbs that I left
Found to be fruitful and frugal
Found all alone and quite bereft.

Found in this ambiguous state
Found to be neither good nor bad
Found by love to be a lightweight
Found not a Don Juan or a cad.

Found to have hobbled feet of clay
Found to possess two paper wings
Found humbly able to convey
My parts and all their hidden strings.

All Crowns Fade To Silver

SILVER LURKS BENEATH US,
buried 'neath our tresses,
where time serenely stalks,
entwining in our locks,
until argent glints bloom
upon this noble loom
where mortal souls quiver,
all crowns fade to silver.

GHOST LOAD

SHE SHOOTS ME EACH DAY WITH HER
smile,
a perfect precious shell of joy,
trajectory beyond denial,
jacketed with a charmed alloy.

It crosses the gap between us,
shortest distance between two points,
targeting my nascent lust
accurately as it anoints

my breast with its sudden impact
instantly puncturing my heart,
fragmenting my very spirit
leaving a wound that won't depart.

Then I see it was fired indifferently,
a ghost load with no real velocity.

BEDSIDE SOPHISTICATE

PUTTING HANDS UPON HER CANCER,
trying not to shudder against
this gesture the only answer
to her whimper for pain to rest.

Then every time trying to speak,
throat pulling tight as a clenched fist,
overwhelmed by a fate so bleak
and dreading to give her a kiss.

Feeling the moment drawing near,
a darksome, unrelenting tide,
restless, impatient, full of fear
like a groom demanding his bride.

Then her last plea came from her eyes,
a look unbearably hopeless
as the reaper chose to baptize
her countenance with fierce anguish.

Stumbling back against peeling wall,
knocking over a hardwood chair,

shocked how so utterly banal

that death struck all and was not rare.

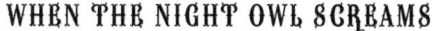

DOWNSTREAM

IS THIS WHAT'S LEFT DOWNSTREAM OF LIFE,
this vague, hollow uncertainty,
these dregs of fifty years of strife
and swirls of latent urgency.

Is this the pool downstream of joys
where all sorrows and angst collects,
the dreams melancholy destroys
and cesspit of yearly regrets.

Is this justice downstream of hurt,
the payoff for the uninspired,
the dirt for those who can't avert
being unloved and unadmired.

Is this the lake where failure flows
and self-pity endlessly crows.

YOUR HURT

I FEEL THE PULSING OF YOUR PAIN,
the homily of all your hurt,
the shame that swims in every vein,
the agony you can't avert.

I hear your every dark whisper
under a hushed uncaring night,
the damages that still blister
and leave you angry at your fright.

I see violence in what you pen,
a harsh, existential torture
of self-inflicted harms that rend
and tear up all hope can conjure.

Your hurt is vast and powerful
a demon most unmerciful.

WITH ONE FOOT ARCHED

IF SHE JUST SLEPT HER LIFE AWAY
would anyone really miss her,
she asks herself this everyday
when hopelessness says surrender.

If she just walked away from life
would her family know she left,
she ponders this most every night
when rejection leaves her bereft.

If she just disappeared one morn
would her few friends notice at all,
she thinks this when she is forlorn
and loneliness clutches with gall.

She imagines she's on a ledge
with one foot arched and her soul parched
about to cross despair's dark edge.

PUPPETEER

ARE YOU THE PUPPET OR THE PUPPETEER
one sister asked the one tied to her strings
or are you just merely a strange sightseer
who came here to witness what sunlight brings.

Tell me, are you the master or the slave
the other girl asked this odd enigma,
this plain strange doll that chose to misbehave
despite also sporting four stigmata.

Are you only here just to torture us
they pleaded loudly but to no avail
now fearing that they'd lost their minds' trust
to this eldritch construct of wood and nail.

Abruptly they severed his primary cord
and showed no surprise as he opened eyes
and murmured the first all too shocking word.

CHAPTER SIX

FEMALE ENERGIES

THE DOUBTS

SOME DAYS SHE CAN'T DENY THE DOUBTS
that cling like dusk's sticky shadows,
turning her into one who pouts
whenever trees release their crows.

Some days she runs from all the doubts
that persecute and threaten her,
chasing like mobs of village louts
demanding that she surrender.

Some days she succumbs to the doubts
that deluge and engulf her soul,
snuffing out all of her hope's shouts,
stripping away all her control.

She craves freedom from disbelief
that treats her welfare like a thief.

RED ACOLYTE

SHE IS THE LAST RED ACOLYTE,
this pale and gentle, hybrid girl,
a daughter born in candlelight
to French tourist and his young churl.

Abandoned at monastery,
the only female among boys,
a childhood most solitary,
never knowing laughter or toys.

Blue acolytes will become priests
and green the finest gardeners,
yellow are cooks that prepare feasts,
rare red girls and other martyrs.

She's reached the age of ascendance
and must decide to leave, or hide
among these walls of repentance.

BARBED WIRE AND BUTTERCUPS

SHE'S LIKE BARBED WIRE AND
buttercups,
so sharp and dangerous outside,
but within a radiant flux,
a blossoming and amber bride.

Life pulls her will, stretching it taut
and girds it with bristling sharpness
so much she feels confined and caught
and desperate to escape darkness.

At times her beauty feels like rust,
a brittle alloy that time plucks,
unmasking joy, turning to dust
just like barbed wire and buttercups.

AN AFRICAN

AN AFRICAN ONCE SAID TO ME
"my suffering is only mine
and not a dish I'd share with he
whose grief sprung naught of my bloodline."

The African was not angry
as she whispered through a sad grin
that I could never wear her skin
no I could never wear her skin.

SHE RISES

THE PAIN IS SO GREAT SHE RISES,
she rises up majestically
with none of life's compromises,
beyond her flesh's enmity.

She rises to escape restraints
like chains of sharp barbed agony,
she rises to outdistance fates
that judge her to be unworthy.

Her arms outstretched she rises high,
feeling complete, at peace at last,
she rises on a final sigh
casting off all her clinging past.

Like a beam of pearly moonlight
she rises free of earth's dark bite.

SHE'S STUCK

SHE'S STUCK IN BED INSIDE HER HEAD,
feeling too tired to move her limbs,
avoiding life and its dire dread,
exhausted by all of fate's whims.

She feels desperately alone
like some drifter on a park bench
in a broadcast of Twilight Zone
where she's a trapped immortal wretch.

She does not have the will to try
and can't think of a reason why
chance always demands she not cry
when failing to ascend the sky.

The weight of her damning despair
shackles her soul with a harsh toll
much more than mortal flesh can bear.

SHE WAS SAD BUT FILLED WITH MOJO

SHE WAS SAD BUT FILLED WITH MOJO,
you know the one, with dripping eyes,
drinking booze laced with cold cocoa,
spinning spells as she softly cries.

Another lonely Friday night,
another lover on the lamb,
crafting her hoard of magic spite
that she would inhale by the gram.

Her beauty undeniable
and her talents beyond compare
but charms are unreliable
when played upon deception's lyre.

Another draught of life's dark brine
that takes the piss out of her bliss
like doleful, melancholy wine.

She Is The Night

SHE IS THE NIGHT, SWEET EBONY,
naked, unapologetic,
the forest's mauve, musky lover,
mist and loam and desire made flesh.

Mother of shadowy creatures,
sister to smiling silver moon,
adorned by sparkling whispering stars,
her mane, loving sable blanket.

Her kiss is soothing and tender,
imparting a most wholesome joy,
tickling the soul, kneading the heart
healing with somnific embrace.

Born of celestial twilight
she is the dark, she is the night.

SHE SLIPS AWAY

AT ODD MOMENTS SHE SLIPS AWAY
severing from normality
and all of the familiar truths
shackling her to reality.

She slips away when she is bored
or life becomes too tedious,
requiring irksome, mundane chores
to and fro through the same old doors.

When sad I see she slips away
beyond the borders of all worlds
into a realm of peaceful dreams
where all her happiness unfurls.

She slips away, going astray
a little more each passing day.

SHE ASKS HERSELF

SHE ASKS HERSELF THE THOUSANDTH TIME
why am I cursed to be alone
as if the oracle of wine
was some wise and respected tome.
She asks herself holding back tears
why fate is so harshly unfair
and why across the endless years
finding a gentle man is rare.
She asks herself upon midnight
when chimes the loneliest of hours
why must the spurned suffer this bite
as all of life bitters and sours.

SHE'S AWARE

SHE'S AWARE THAT THIS SOUNDS CRAZY
to all of the normal people,
but you're all dreamlike and hazy,
unformed, unaware, and fetal.

At least that's how she sees the world
and all that is surrounding her,
disturbing motes faintly unfurled
and alive as a cadaver.

Logic tells her she must beware
this frightening, shady mystery
and strange vision she'll never share,
she's afraid that this sounds crazy.

SHE IS THE NIGHT

SHE IS SAPPHIRE AND LAVENDER,
she is the shadow's tender bite,
she is midnight's ambassador,
she's saturnine, she is the night.

Her mood is black habiliment
worn with a suave and sable flair,
a glowing azure filament
that freckles her ebony hair.

I asked her to consider me
but she denied my amber plea
saying her love defies all light
and shuns the sun eternally.

She lurks just beyond my daydreams
where dawn kisses morning's wishes
and she whispers from these dark seams.

SHADOWGIRL

S WEET SHADOWGIRL YOU SHADOW ME
in shades of serendipity,
flickering just outside my sight
and fueling my serenity.

Sweet shadowgirl so willowy
with curves refined yet billowy,
I feel your undulating soul
slipping over my destiny.

Sweet shadowgirl posing at dusk
outlined in sundown's amber musk,
spicy, and dark, and alluring,
tithing kisses light as a hush.

PALE LOVE

PALE LOVERS ARE THE STRANGEST BREED
   lush libertines with lilac skin
born of unsympathetic seed
yet most alluring of all kin.

They pose with statuesque beauty
soft and silver beneath the moon
whisp'ring night's sweetest entreaty
that mesmerizes as you swoon.

Their touch like warm alabaster
their gaze the milk of every want
their breath the wine of joy vaster
than any and all enchantment.

Creatures of sultry ivory
forever ever haunting me.

LAVENDER SIRENS

I SEE THEM GATHER ON THE SHORE
as purple fingers of sunlight
reach across the horizon's door
to warn them of the end of night.

Their forms are cool and willowy,
lovely, gauzy, moonlight specters
with midnight locks so billowy
and laughter like wispy vapors.

They call to me upon the dawn
and yes my will almost submits
to sweet eyes that both flirt and fawn
and unbearably sultry lips.

Three mercurial temptresses
magenta maids enchanted shades
whose beauty traps and possesses.

CLOAKED

S HE'S STRIPPED HERSELF OF EVERY FEAR,
  she's shed her thick skin of worries,
wearing only the moon's veneer
before starting eldritch journeys.

She's naked in the wilderness
of her desire's intensity,
boldly embracing nature's bliss
in shy, shadowy ecstasy.

She stretches arms and arches neck
and yawns so luxuriously,
the first step of this daring trek
as her heart beats furiously.

She's cloaked herself in silky night
and slowly her spirit takes flight.

HAPPY BIRTHDAY

EACH BIRTHDAY IS HER VERY FIRST
and she gives herself one cupcake
because she knows that she is cursed
with a dark vow she cannot break.

Each year she stands before mirror
holding pastry with one candle
burning 'til it must disappear
into frosting like a vandal.

And with a shocking force of will
she does not lick or taste this treat
destined for some distant landfill
as anything else is a cheat.

For years before her mother died
through her childhood she understood
beauty requires she be deprived.

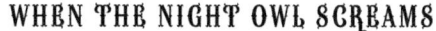

UNLOCKED

*U*NLOCKED AT LAST, SHE BROKE THE
chain
and she is finally waking up,
no longer afraid of the pain
of drinking from fate's hopeful cup.

Unshackled defying boundaries,
no longer beholden to one
that treated her like mere sundries
acquired and shelved out of the sun.

Unfettered by any borders
felt in spirit and flesh and bone,
beyond any harsh man's orders,
free to make choices of her own.

The roads are wide and inviting
her soul now glowing and gliding.

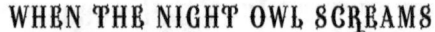

CHRYSALIS

FATE STRIPPED AWAY HER WOMANHOOD
with a sharpened stainless steel blade
for banes that could not be withstood
and demons she could not evade.

Supplanting loveliness with scars,
such ugliness from gentle hands,
when sickness is replaced by cures,
women are sacrificial lambs.

And thus she chose a path of pain
knowing her true soul was cocooned,
allowing creation free reign,
imbedding beauty on her wound.

Reborn beneath an artist's eye
blossoming like a butterfly.

THE CORNER

S HE'S STUCK NOW, RIGHT AT THE CORNER,
halfway from there halfway to here,
unable to progress further,
unable to overcome fear.

She's crossing the dividing line
between before and into now,
but is not ready to divine
the answers to why, when, and how.

She's reaching forward into time,
phasing from one life to the next,
unsure if this strange pantomime
is what her true desires reflect.

Hugging her corner desperately
and poising to pull herself free.

Its Raining

ITS RAINING NOW, THAT'S WHAT SHE HEARS,
even though the sun shines outside,
a dark shower of pain and fear
like a grieving and jilted bride.

Its raining though she sees blue skies
overhead as she walks this park,
she feels the drip of thick wet sighs
while others think she's on a lark.

Its raining she can smell the musk
of soggy flesh, fur, bark, and soil
though sunbathers defy the muck
her mind knows is drowning her soul.

She's damned and haunted by this rain
no one can see
no one but she
this storm that rages in her brain.

GLOWING

S HE GLOWS WITH AN INTENSE SORROW,
a harsh, baleful luminescence
that radiates from her marrow,
quintessence of adolescence.

Daily she wrings her hands and grieves,
eyes spilling rivers of deep pain,
dampening her overused sleeves
with all the angst that comes with blame.

The burns of social awkwardness,
the fire of sneer and snide remark,
the torture of ungainliness,
each and every accusing smirk.

Locker-hallways gauntlets of shame
filled with whispers that mock and maim.

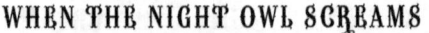

AWAY

SOME DAYS SHE WANTS TO FADE AWAY,
away from every fickle day,
to strip off all of life's dark pain,
and leave through some magic archway.

She needs something that will allay
all of her current hurts and aches,
promising to lead her astray
to soothing rivers and ripe grapes.

She simply wants to go someplace,
to slip into this golden haze,
warming her soul as it sashays
and melts into dusk's amber glaze.

Away, away, to far away
dissolving thus without a fuss
escaping every yesterday.

LES SAVEURS DU DEUIL

S HE GRIEVES FOR ALL THAT SHE HAS LOST
but not so much that she despairs
the caustic captivating cost
that fill her hot and burning tears.

She cries for those no longer here,
feeling their absence in her heart
but won't succumb to crippling fear
that threatens to tear her apart.

She suffers all mortal anguish
feeling like life's own carrion
refusing to let death vanquish
visions of loved ones now long gone.

Misfortune's weight may burden her
but its sweet taste can't make her slake
this harsh thirst for hate's dark liquor.

WHERE ALL GOOD FAILS

EVERYWHERE SHE RUNS, SHE'S CAUGHT,
everywhere she flees, she's trapped,
bound by strong chains of fear and thought,
quickly hauled off like one kidnapped.

No matter the path, she is found,
no matter the way, she is kept
by feelings that unfairly bound
her willpower as she just wept.
Every direction, she's stopped,
every bearing, she's thwarted
by restraints that can't be unlocked
by any prince that she's courted.

These are not happy fairy tales
but life's sad and enduring tropes
where all good fails, evil prevails
and all that's left are wispy hopes.

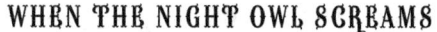

CRAZYLANDS

REFUGEE FROM THE CRAZYLANDS,
covered in the dust of deranged,
she is not one who understands
why her sanity was estranged

from all those she once knew and loved,
from everything that she held dear,
feeling like a small child just shoved
onto the subway tracks of fear

and now she's back inside the world
exposed to a harsh, unbarred sun,
her consciousness has just uncurled
loathing freedom's dominion.

This tidal wave of normalcy
erodes her will like acid rain
with a burning lucidity
so conventionally arcane.

Breathing pale ordinary air,
drinking a rational routine,

eating life's grey and common fare
with veins emptied of Thorazine.

She wonders why no one can see
simplicity's depravity
this nightmare of just being free.

LISTEN TO THE PIMP

L ISTEN TO THE PIMP, HEAR HER RAP,
her mod-atomic hair so rad,
she's the mom of the raw palm-slap,
revolution boots scream she's bad.

Listen to the pimp, she's the queen
of all that crawls through Neverland,
her blood type UM, ultra-mean
giving fate the back of her hand.

Listen to the pimp, she skateboards
across bleeding, broken concrete,
she's the bitch-goddess of dark hordes
of walking, talking teenage meat.

Listen to the pimp, listen to her roar
vixen with a twist, dancing with furor.

ABOUT THE ARTIST
CHRIS MARS

Chris Mars (born April 26, 1961) is an American painter and musician. He was the drummer for the seminal Minneapolis alternative-rock band the Replacements from 1979 to 1990, then joined the informal supergroup Golden Smog before beginning a solo career. Mars more or less left music behind in the late '90s in order to concentrate on his artwork.

His painting style, examples of which grace all of his album covers, is marked by nightmarish landscapes and grotesque, distorted figures. He draws inspiration from his older brother's struggle with schizophrenia.

He generally likes to use oils or pastels, although he ventures into other media, like acrylic and scratchboard. He created a 13-minute animated film about his work titled The Severed Stream.

His work, which has fetched prices of more than $30,000, has been shown throughout the United States and Canada. He has had solo exhibitions at Billy Shire Fine Arts, The Erie Art Museum, The Minneapolis Institute of Arts, The Steensland Museum, Coker Bell Gallery, and the Mesa Arts Center.

View more of Chris' art at www.chrismarspublishing.com

ABOUT THE POET

Michael H. Hanson has written four collections of poetry: *Autumn Blush* and *Jubilant Whispers* whose second editions will soon be published by Racket River Press (an imprint of Copper Dog Publishing LLC), *Dark Parchments: Midnight Curses and Verses* published by Moon-Dream Press (an imprint of Copper Dog Publishing LLC), and *When The Night Owl Screams* also published by Moon-Dream Press. He has written and sold over two dozen individual poems to various periodicals, magazines, anthologies, and online venues over the past fifteen years.

Michael is the Creator of the Sha'Daa shared-world action/fantasy anthology series currently consisting of *Sha'Daa: Tales of The Apocalypse, Sha'Daa: Last Call, Sha'Daa: Pawns, Sha'Daa: Facets, Sha'Daa: Inked,* and the soon to be released *Sha'Daa: Toys* all published by MoonDream Press.

Copper Dog Publishing LLC

OUR IMPRINTS

SCIENCE FICTION, HORROR AND FANTASY

POETRY

Pumpkin Hill Press

CHILDRENS' TITLES

To find out more about our imprints
and our upcoming releases, visit our website:
www.CopperDogPublishing.com
or our Facebook page:
www.facebook.com/copperdogpublishing

www.ingramcontent.com/pod-product-compliance
Lightning Source LLC
Chambersburg PA
CBHW060748180626
46818CB00002B/504